An Incomplete Story of a Whole Person

Copyright © 2010 by Sunny Love

All rights reserved. No part of this publication may be reproduced, stored in a retrieval system, or transmitted, in any form or by any means, electronic, mechanical, photocopying, recording, or otherwise, without the prior permission of Sunny Love.

Library of Congress Cataloging-in-Publication Data by Literary Works applied for.

ISBN 978-1-60458-725-8

Printed in the United States of America

Contents

Forward	v
Acknowledgements	vi
Introduction	8
Poem	11
A World Gone Different Why?	13
The Broken Child Within	16
Tripping Down Memory Lane	19
My Feelings About Intimacy	23
Still Faking The Passion	25
I Believed Because I Changed the World Would Embrace Me	28
I Shared Chapters, Four, Five and Six With my Husband	32
The Road Was Not Easy	36
Was I stupid or Just Obedient to the Word?	39

Teaching a New Style of Living	43
Learning Obedience to the Word	45
Rashon's Story	49
Inside a Mother's Heart	54
How Do I Truly Share With You What It Has Been Like?	61
The Day I Asked for a Raise	66
No One Informed Us It Would Be So Hard	69
The World That Believed That We Were Not Worth Much	71
How Do You Keep Going Against All Odds?	75
They Called Me Ms. Whitney	77
It's a New Day	79
Just Because I Believed Things Would Change	82
Life is Truly a Journey	85
The Rewards of Moving Forward	87
It Really Does Not Matter What They Believe	92
When My Eyes Became Opened	96

An Incomplete Story of a Whole Person
By Sunny Love

Forward

Sunny created trainings in the area of re-entry skills, employment readiness, circles of support and mediation. She had facilitated over 1500 hours of trainings and workshops prepared herself to be able to accomplish that work by filling her calendar with monthly trainings in those areas. Finally, she found herself still 13 years later, well versed and educated to work with a very diverse population knowing she had supported so many individuals in making their transition from a life of self-destruction to complete freedom of self. So many of the men, women and children had to endure such devastating lives, some things even for her she found to have been worse than what she had gone through. She said so many of us always believe our lives were harder than anyone else's, but that is never really the case; there is always someone worst off than you are.

Acknowledgements

This book took a lot of personal soul searching and letting go of painful memories and nightmares that will probably continue haunting us until the day we leave this earth. I have been blessed to let go of a lot of the stress that I had previously let rule my life. A life that had been filled with so much discord that one had come to believe that was all life entailed. How little we allow our brains to take in when we have lived a life filled with half truths, and never questioning the very ones who fed us most of that garbage.

Throughout most of my past life I believed almost everything negative a person had said about me and never even remembered trying to tap into the goodness I had felt within. Today is a new day and life I know will never be the same for me, why? Because I know that I have value and I really do know what it means to value myself above giving all my power over to someone else.

I am so thankful to my children who have always stood by my side and have continuously been a huge part of my life, yet today I do not just live to be their mother. I live because I desire to leave a legacy for them to remember me by. That life will have been filled with me loving myself as richly as I love them.

To my husband whom I have struggled with loving as well, because I had to learn how to love me in order to be a wife to him too! The Lord showed me how to be capable of doing both.

Introduction

How do I began to say to all of those who did not know my past that I am sorry for the pain they may have felt when they found out that I had lived through such horrendous and painful childhood memories. Yet there are so many who will never understand how one could even be so honest about sharing what had happened to them in their past. And I do not even have a problem with them not understanding, because some of the things that happened even I would never be able to give meaning to its causes.

How long does one live with such darkness in their lives all those years and then one day came to realize that it was time to share it, and share it so openly. You see my friends I am free from my past for the very first time in my whole life. I tried to even explain what that felt like within the Church and I still do not believe they even get it. When you have a burning testimony that is alive within your Soul and it needs to get out, and when I think back on the Scripture that says they were saved by the words of their testimonies, it meant so very much to me – it was a call to the silent voice within my soul.

Throughout my whole life I had tried to understand why I never liked myself as a child and especially as an adult. Well there were too many dark secrets hiding deep down within my core that needed to be set free. Whom the Lord sets free is free indeed, and what a blessing those words were to my Spirit.

Have you ever wanted to surrender something that kept you bound but you did not know how to let it go for fear of what the world might think? Well the world I learned did not give me my soul and it could not take it away and when I learned this as a true feeling of freedom, it was as though I could taste it and the flavor of it seasoned my mouth with such a sweet savory essence. I felt as though for the first time if freedom had a flavor I was sampling it right at that very moment.

Many of my friends spoke with me about how I did not share with anyone how my life had truly changed so drastically from where I once was – and I informed them that I did not desire to be seen as bragging. Since *"Robbed of a Childhood, Raped by the System"* my life has become so very different even for me I have experienced wisdom beyond my years. The kind of wisdom that only the Lord could have given me insight into its very existence.

Once I got out of that lifestyle of living too fast and dealing with a different set of friends I had to start everything over, trying to create a new lifestyle. A world built on purity and truthfulness that I had so longed to share, but had too much shame buried within the core of my being. You see when you place the little devil deep within the dungeon where no one can see him, if you allow him to get free my belief was, and then the world would hate me too!

Where do I begin to share with the world how to do a true transformation in their lives, one that will never let you be the person you had lived from birth until middle age being? I am now 57 years old, never believing since momma died when I was eleven that I would live past the age of 34, just like her. My how wrong I was to believe that my death would come as abruptly as hers did.

I want to say thanks to so many men, women and youth who truly have made an impact in my life by sharing their journeys with me. All of us have done this very special work together and had it not been for my privilege of working with them would I be as free from my own ghosts as I am today.

Be blessed, be encouraged and never look back; knowing that there is a brighter tomorrow on the other side of the rainbow, but you have to desire to find the pot of gold hidden there for yourselves.

POEM

WHY DARE TO DREAM
By Mary Whitney

Today I Dare to Dream because I knew the purpose of my calling so, Why Should I Dare to Dream I don't believe I should momma always said I would never amount to anything.

So Why Should I Dare to Dream because daddy was never around and I was considered just his maybe, maybe I was or maybe I wasn't.

So Why Should I Dare to Dream, to dream no one ever seemed to understand me because I never even understood me.

So Why Should I Dare to Dream, to dream when all I can ever remember is my step-father and mother fighting all the time. Cursing and cutting, hitting and missing and I always thought it was my fault. Maybe if I had not been born they would not fight so much? Guess I will never know the answer to that question cause momma died when I was eleven years old.

Why Should I Dare to Dream cuz this house is not a home, and I feel so all alone. Why did momma have to pass on I'm so mixed up who do I talk to? Where can I go? My I just don't know.

Why Should I Dare to Dream when the pain inside makes me turn mean. Where do I go, why do I have to be there with those people I didn't really know.

Why Should I Dare to Dream when all I wanted to do was scream. DeAnn cursed me out morning, noon and night. The language she used became my new vocabulary.

So Why Should I Dare to Dream when cursing had become a way of life for me. I began to hate myself for the new words I had acquired.

Why Should I Dare to Dream when I look back over my life and I think of all the things I have gone through and survived that is Why I Dare to Dream. Today I say to you it is a bright new morning and until you begin to care for yourselves, you cannot truly take care of anyone else.

Chapter One

A World Gone Different
Why?

For years after writing my book *"Robbed of a Childhood, Raped by the System"* by Sunny Love, I was still filled with rage and anguish over the why me's. Why did I have to be the one to be raped from the age of six until eleven? Why did momma have to die and go on to heaven and leave me behind? Why was I the one along with my brother to be picked up and taken off to Indianapolis to live with my father and step-mother, both of whom I really did not know that well.

So many why me's, I had going through my head. Well you will have to read "Robbed of a Childhood, Raped by the System" by **Sunny Love** for yourselves and you share with me what you thought as you read the book. I will be waiting with arms wide open to hear back from as many of you as possible. Go to www.sunnylovetalkshow.com .

When several of the people I knew read my book, they shared with me that they had read it in a day; others said I never put your book down and I wanted to know what was going to happen in the next chapters. Some asked me why I did not share with the world how much I had done since I was no longer the person I once was, but how could I share with them even though it seemed as though I was this strong, powerful self-directed woman. Deep down inside I was still feeling lost and all alone, afraid to still come out of the shadows of death.

You see everyone, when you have given up so much of whom you believed you were created to be, there is really not much left to change the face of your hidden shame. Yes, I could help other men, women and children, find their way out of the wilderness; but I was still hidden within my own torment. Not really ready to accept for my own life that which I was qualified to teach others so readily. Therefore, deep down inside this way of teaching left me with feelings of hypocrisy.

I have done some amazing things since never looking back and picking up old behaviors. Some of those things consisted of my creating an organization called "Women Planting Seeds" whose mission is ***"Being Committed to Changing Lives and Providing Second Chances"*** for those who many times who were left in the shadows without the proper resources to change their own dire situations as well. So many of whom I found myself easy to relate to and tap into the same sort of feelings and self defeated purposes they were living. I shared with them that I knew why they felt challenged and that was all right. And that if they would allow me to share with them some of the things I had learned about my own self-defeating behaviors they too could live a new and changed lifestyle. One they never ever believed possible too, oh yes, I shared with them it would take some work. But all any work truly consisted of is first of all a willingness to allow ourselves to be changed. You see change is always possible if at first we just believe.

Chapter Two

The Broken Child Within

I was broken from the core and did not even know what was happening to me. All throughout my life I never knew why I could not fit in with the rest of the world. I learned a lot about life through reading, not through being taught because my mother died when I was only eleven years old. My father was not known to me, except the times he would come and visit me on a remote Tennessee farm, where I lived with my mother, stepfather and our blended family of children. There were twelve of us in all, but none of them were his children. Just my brother Bennie and I would be taken away from that farm and carried off to Indianapolis.

When I looked back over my life and thought about all the things that I had lived through it was amazing that I turned out to be a sort of complete person some know me as today. The world sees me now as a well rounded fully qualified person, capable of so many things – then why is it so hard for me to operate continuously at that level, without wearing feeling of being torn apart at the seams, which keeps me wondering if ever I will have complete happiness before I leave this world.

I am married living with my current husband of 15 years, continuously fighting off feelings of distrust in the relationship, fully capable of teaching others to move forward pass their issues; while at the same time holding on to many of my own insecurities. Yet deep down inside I knew living for the Lord that I had to let go of those thoughts realizing that those old ways held no weight within me anymore. I am a Christian and living a life filled with brokenness was no longer what caused me to awaken in my right mind the following morning. This new way of being was filled with excitement and living water rushing through my veins. No longer did I have to live a life of lies faking the grove, but it is not the sort of grove I once was able to move too!

So many might ask me how was I able to feel the beat of a new music, the kind that plays deep down in your soul and no cords are being played at that very moment. I could share with them I felt joy deep down in my soul. And no it had nothing to do with past songs or rhythms that excited me, such as the men or women who once called out your name because they loved the way you danced or because they believed you had the gift of movement. But now my life is filled with the music of the Spirit, which grounds me and keeps my feet from slipping or moving to the wrong sort of tunes. No longer could anyone accuse me of coming alive because I was dressed half naked and moving to the vulgarity of degrading language within the songs of today's world.

Today each and every morning I awaken encouraging myself to leave behind past destructive behaviors and I am filled with fruitful words to help lift someone else up, especially the men, women and youth I serve. I do not have time to be miserable, or even spread that sort of discord to anyone else, nor do I have time to cry; but I do have time to serve another. This way of living is as normal to me now as the fresh morning dew I smell each day, filled with thought of praise and gratitude for being able to life up His holy name.

Chapter Three

Tripping Down Memory Lane

As I sat back in my home where some would share they were waiting to exhale. I found myself throughout a lot of my life waiting to breathe. So much so that I started having what was called panic attacks. Many would ask me what the attacks were like. Or why did I believe I was going to stop breathing? If I knew the answer to those questions, maybe I would not have had a panic attack in the first place, but when you do not even understand the cause of something yourself, how could you explain the experience? What I really did not understand is that my life had truly been transformed, and the things I once did I knew were no longer an option for my current style of living. Why, because I did not even desire to be the girl/woman many knew as Sunny! Sunny was a bad girl, one that went through the motions that came with acts of love, but it really was not love. Love to me meant you felt special and you desired to be held or caressed. As a woman I have never known what it really felt like to feel the chills of passion running through my body. All I ever knew was feelings of squinting up and trying not to show how tense I was when touched.

At times I would ask myself, how do other women respond so lovingly to their husbands/man? Why would they even desire to be touched by those men? Were they really in love, or were all women just pretending to please their partners, I would like to ask someone one day, and look them in their eyes while they shared their answer. Then I would know deep down in my heart that their feelings were real. Often times I did find myself wondering what it would feel like to look forward to having the man I love take me in his arms and whisk me off my feet.

We can break our necks to see the soap operas and what was going to happen on the next episode, especially if the day before there was a hot steamy romantic scene. There were times I caught myself saying, when are they going to stop messing up the best relationships by having the wives have an affair with another man on the show? Or the man having an adulterous relationship with some other mans wife.

In this world we live in today with everyone and everything moving so fast, when will we slow our rolls? Will there come a time in this lifetime of mine that marriage will truly be considered precious and holy? People ask me all the time why do I desire to live a saved and holy life, it feels so natural for me to share with them that since I stopped being Sunny, that is the only kind of lifestyle that seems right. What I cannot explain to them is when did I loose Mary and become Sunny, and I have never desired to pick up any part of my past.

What has kept me living the life I live today is all the self-help, affirmations, and empowerment training sessions that I have been blessed to teach.

Why, because in order to teach those healthy behaviors to others I had to clean out the broken areas of my own life. You see in becoming a Christian, one that does not play with the Lord, but by choice I choose to be that living example. One that truly does live that holy life that is filled with love from the heart; as I share that agape sort of love with those I teach. In my new world there is no such thing as faking it until we make it to the next level. You either surrender to change or you fall back into old habits, because what is working on the inside will eventually come into operation on the outside and start creating its own existence all over again.

I believe by living the life I live today, I am really transformed and a new creature came into existence; not to be hidden ever again. We are capable of operating at a different capacity, and born of a new model, filled with life giving transferring energy to all those we teach. Now we are purposefully designed and solidified in giving a new lifestyle for the world to grab hold of – this I believe is what the Lord desires us to share, because perfect love casts out all fear; and I have learned through much listening that the Lord desires for us to prosper as our souls does prosper in Him.

If we allow ourselves to be poor in our spirits, then we will be poor in prosperity as well. You see richness does not only come with a pocketful of money. It comes from the healthy core of our very existence. You see what many of us take for granted, such as: learned skills, others never were blessed to be trained appropriately in them to begin with. Therefore, it is my belief that when I was sitting at the back of the church that I so willingly came to the front of today. Is that the Lord made a lasting transformation in my life, so that I might be blessed and unselfish enough to share that knowledge with others – so they might see His richness and learn through experience to share it ever so freely with their family and friends as well?

Not all of us were taught how to live healthy lifestyles, so much of the time we operated in survival mode and never learned to stabilize our lives. For many of us life just happened and we were just blessed from birth to be current in our existence as we live our lives today. Then one day along came someone willing to share their blessings freely with others. If we can continue this sort of release, then our world will be a much brighter place for our children/grandchildren to live. For the Lord says "my people perish because of a lack of knowledge", so when you have more than the next person – what is the harm in sharing what you were freely given or born with?

Chapter Four

My Feelings about Intimacy

I never learned how to truly deal with my feelings of inadequacy or my distorted feelings in learning how to deal with intimacy in a relationship. Why? Because sex for me had always been associated with feelings of shame and ugliness and so therefore, it was always compared by me with feelings of force and not a willingness to give into sweet emotions, those kind that come with someone giving of themselves freely while having sex. I do not ever recall a time when I could think about allowing someone to caress and hold me tightly within their arms. It was too painful to think about sex in that sort of way.

So all throughout my life I would look in the mirror and see myself as this shame ridden person who desired to be someone else who was not tarnished, or who had never allowed anyone to touch her in a bad way. But because of having been forced by my stepbrothers to have sex with them, I could never be the virgin I so dreamed of being, embracing my husband with pride in my heart. As a child that had already been determined for me, by someone I never desired to take me that way in the first place. So not only as a child was I filled with rage, then came my teenage years, where I was forced by my boyfriend to have sex with him at age seventeen and I became pregnant through our first sexual encounter.

Once again I had found myself detesting the fact of having someone touch me in a sexual manner. Therefore what was there for me to look forward to during intimacy? I had been robbed of the pure thoughts of what the possibility could ever be like.

Then I ended up marrying the very boyfriend who had raped me and impregnated me with my first child because I was ashamed of what the world would think of me as an unwed mother. Being the country girl that I was, that was not going to be the route I wanted to take either.

Then came the times when I was considered a working woman and there definitely was no room for intimacy during those encounters!

Chapter Five

Still Faking the Passion

Today what my husband does not know is that I still do not know how to allow myself to enjoy having sex with him or anyone else, for fear of enjoying something that is demented or wrong. I want to share my feelings with him, but I am afraid he might not understand or blame himself for my pain. Yet I know that none of those feelings are his fault.

So I just act as thought I am satisfied with our intimate times together. I believe my fear is due in large part, because of my own insecurities of trusting anyone when they share with me that they love me. I have always believed that I will never be able to trust anyone, especially not men, and no I do not desire to be in an intimate relationship with a woman. It is my thoughts that it is because I was violated as a child by the very men, I should have been able to trust, that I will never trust the sincerity of any relationship. Especially since my own stepbrothers and then my step-father, violated me, and if you are questioning my faithfulness to my husband, do not think that way; because I have been faithful throughout our whole marriage because I desire to go to heaven one day and I do love him in my own mixed up way. I just cannot seem to force myself to trust him, even though I would like to, because he also hurt me many times prior to where we are in our relationship today.

My husband and I are much closer than we ever have been to having the kind of open and honest relationship I have so desired for so many years. But we are still not where I would like for us to be, because I believe he is afraid of putting all his trust into being devoted to one woman. He informs me all the time that he loves his wife and has never been unfaithful, but he keeps talking to one woman from his past on the phone quite a bit. Therefore, until that changes I will never fully put my whole mind, body and trust into this relationship, but I will continue being faithful. I told him, because of his actions sometimes I wonder if I should just be alone and see what it feels like just to do me, he said no, and I do not desire to hurt my husband. So for now we have decided to stay committed to one another in our marriage and work through our little insecurity.

We had previously tried to have several conversations about separating, but he says he loves his wife and does not desire to be apart, and the Bible that I follow as faithfully as I can, informs me that if an unsaved husband desires to stay with his saved wife – then I must keep myself from violating my marriage and not push him out of the home. So if I desire to be led by the Holy Spirit to do the right thing in the eyes of God – to put my husband away is not an option.

I have learned a lot about establishing a relationship not only with the Lord, but between two people and some of those ingredients are: A relationship is built on trust, love and understanding. It is not one-sided, and it always takes more than one party desires to create, which is, why we have decided to keep working at ours until we get it right. Life in part is what we make of it, and if we are both willing to do all that we can to stay committed then that is what we are going to do!

Chapter Six

I Believed Because I Changed, the World Would Embrace Me

It just doesn't happen like that. And how quick I found this out and it first started between my husband and me. At times I thought just because I had the Bible as my way of escaping the world that he would follow suit. And when this did not happen I lost a little hope in our relationship and at times found myself going to the my Pastor complaining about us being unequally yoked. Oh yes, there are passages in the Bible that speaks of being yoked together with those who do not carry our same beliefs. This was seen through my own eyes to mean that since he would not act the way I wanted him to be that he was now an unequal partner. It was now time for me to come to grips with that shedding off the old self and just priming myself to deal with some uncomfortable feelings.

You see the Lord never said that once we became saved that it would be without pain. I began to realize that those feelings that made me feel weak, was what needed to happen so my inner person could become strong. It is my belief that this became a good thing and that I began to like the person that I was becoming. You see my old person had to change and change only makes us better. That is, if it is putting on layers of peace, love, hope and charity. Because love is not based on the conditions I created it out to be just to satisfy my old self. How do you deal with your moments of not having your own way? Do you believe it just means we can throw that person away and find a newer model that might just work out better for us? Well, if so, I believe you would be setting small expectations on your marriage, and if you do not go through something at that moment. You will be in for a larger issue later on in life or even just a few steps into your next relationship.

We must allow the Lord to work out the kinks in our own distorted view of life. You see what I found out in letting go of my mistaken views is there was a whole new way of being I have never given much thought to! How about you? When I went to Scripture, especially Roman's 12:1 in the King James Version of the Bible it reads: "I beseech you therefore, brethren, by the mercies of God, that *ye* present your bodies a living sacrifice, holy, acceptable unto God, *which is* your reasonable service". Then *verse 2* read: "And be not conformed to this world: but be ye transformed by the renewing of your mind, that ye may prove what is *that* good, and acceptable, and perfect, will of God." As I thought on those Scriptures and believing them directed toward the new person I desired to become. It made me think of how much the Lord had given of Himself that we might have a better life too! I could no longer just expect my husband to change. I had to allow the Lord to work the old beliefs out of me.

Today I offer my body as a living sacrifice to our Lord and Savior and I can go through many more things than I ever believed I was willing to let go of before. I love the new person that I have become and yes I still love my husband very much too! Even though he does not do everything the way I believe I would, he is his own person. I am accountable only for the sinful things I commit and not his and you can believe he is different than he once was too! We both are and we are going to get this right hopefully together.

The world does not embrace me the way I believed that it should either, but that is all right too! As a child growing up I did not have much love and acceptance in the family I was brought up in either. And I learned really fast that all families were not as our family structure had been. It is my belief that when we can stop comparing ourselves and our families to those television shows or someone else's lives then we can truly see life through a new set of lenses. We can let old beliefs and behaviors pass away and allow a new creature to emerge.

In living a life filled with the blessings of the Lord everything that I once took for granted could no longer be a part of who I was being. I am so very glad that I have learned to read the words written in the Bible and put it into application within my current life, and I have never felt more complete than I do today. It has not been easy living this way and no the world does not see you as this beautiful creature. They know that you are different and that the things you once did, you no longer do anymore. I believe they still see me as a shattered model, not measuring up to how they see themselves. But remember since I have never learned to trust anyone, I might not have my eyes wide open, and this is just ones own perception of things, and therefore I ask that you draw your own conclusions to this chapters ending. Because that way you might just find your own humanness being energized too!

Chapter Seven

(I Shared Chapters Four, Five and Six with my Husband)

The night we shared how I felt about intimacy and our relationship through my own eyes and I asked him what he thought. He said "if that is how you see things, then that is just how it is". He never tried to convince me otherwise, he just allowed me to be whom I needed to be. A true expression of self came out that night and I believe it really is a breakthrough in our openness together. You see my husband does not talk to me much to share his own thoughts. But he disagrees, because that is just who he is!

I have often wondered how he has so much to say to that other person who he talks to on the phone sometimes. Yet, he never will tell me the truth about who she is, for fear of my "I believe, leaving our relationship". If he only knew that deep in my heart I am feeling the opposite. I feel that eventually I will get filled with even more doubts about what is being kept a secret and eventually leave. That is if we do not grow old and gray and die with those uncertainties locked up within us. It is my belief that we have both been broken in so many places; we are both afraid of truly opening up to one another all the way. A loss of power I believe as a man is what he fears most, so I must continue to allow him to wear the pants in this relationship.

I am sure some of you will say that I am just being a fool for love. But I can share with you that it is more than that. It is my belief that my husband shows me love in the most effective way he has learned to share that exchange of emotions. We are all so very different and I have yet to meet the perfect man or woman. That is what the Lord has given me inside Him. He is the only perfect person that has ever walked this thing we call earth. The word of the Lord is so pure, clean and true and that perfected side of the Lord is where I would like to find myself just living in until I leave this world.

When I picked up the Bible and began reading it so long ago. One of the major things I took to heart is that as long as I stood on the truth and shared my purest thoughts with my husband. The Lord is the only one in the end that I have to please, and therefore, I give the Lord charge over my life, even more than I surrender to my husband. For the Lord has been my husbandman and I trust in Him with all my heart, soul, mind and body, and some would ask why; and I would say because He first loved me. The Lord has truly never forsaken me, nor has he left me hungry and having to revert back to any of my old ways. And for that I will always be so forever grateful and no matter what the world does to me. I know and believe I can withstand their negativity and harshness. For the love of God has been shown to me in my life, it does not cast me aside because I was/am flawed. And a person's worth is not judged by man, but by your trust and belief in God.

I have shared with many of my friends and those that I have came in contact with, that we should just live the best life we can, and without judgment. Because whom we judge and what we say in that judgment will come back on us one day.

The Lord has been my strength and the very foundation of His words is what I challenge myself to always keep written within the table of my own heart. That I know in all that I do that I might not sin against Him.

When I realized that the Lord had forgiven me of my sinful nature. I have done everything I know humanly possible to share His sort of love with the world as I have gotten to know it. At times I have felt alienated from part of this current world because of my beliefs. But I would not trade this new life I have learned to live for all the gold and rubies I could ever acquire. I have a peace within that I have never known before and I believe only the Lord could have given me this sort of comfort. There is a place in the Lord that nothing or no one can disturb inside of me. I wish I could really explain it, but I know it is pure comfort. That is, if I allow myself to rest in that place. Even when challenged, if I just let go of my painful thoughts the Lord will take me to that place, and yes to my son "Rashon" who at times "say, mom I do not desire to go there right now". Yet in the end he allows me to go there with him too!

Chapter Eight

The Road Was Not Easy

Well so many of those I have known wanted me to share with the world how I got to the point in my life I am at today. They believe it could not have been an easy transformation, and no it was not. I cannot believe myself that I was able to let go of the crack and marijuana, or the cigarettes, but the Lord showed me that I could be forgiven of all of my sins as well. It was a continuous battle within my fleshly desires and the desire to be a new creature, each day as my struggle became more apparent. I read the scriptures over and over to gain a realistic perspective of what those words were saying to my spirit. The battle became harder and harder, but I was determined never to look back, and especially not take a chance on being carted off to jail or even worse prison.

You see the work I once did would never be an option for me anymore and this I knew from the bottom of my heart. I had learned to love the person that I found myself becoming, and I felt special and wholeness was beginning to set in, for once in my life I felt beautiful and whole; truly complete. This style of living was truly rich in essence and I just wanted to not only share it with my children, but with the whole world. I truly believed that if only I could put into a capsule what the Lord had shared with me in His word, whomever life I was blessed to share this new found Source with would be changed forevermore.

Those new experiences were ones I never believed I was worthy of receiving. I had my children, my health and a new man in my life to keep me motivated enough to continue pressing forward. There were days that he and I argued over the smallest things, things that really did not make a lot of sense to me. I found out that I was going through menopause at the time; it made me have feelings of depression, anguish and just plain evilness. When my husband would put the key into the door, I would lay my Bible to the side and promise my Lord that I was not going to be bothered by his tardiness, but I was bothered; and not only that, I was really annoyed and angry.

I found myself striking out at him with a tongue that I was praying for deliverance from, one that had picked up its venomous ways, once again. This is when I really knew something was wrong and I went to the doctor and asked her to prescribe for me some valiums – these I knew would calm me down. But I did not desire to hide my feelings of discord, I wanted to deal with them and stop screaming at my husband. Even though it seemed to me that he was sneaking around talking to a woman he had not cut off conversations with since our marriage. I wanted to have faith in our marriage, believing that I was enough to keep him happy.

Ladies what would you do if monthly you saw your phone bill and your husband was phoning the other woman speaking with her for 30 minutes and sharing with you prior to phoning her that it was time for his break to be over with. Or there were times he would tell me someone else was in the lunch room, which was why he had not phoned me sooner. Yet when you saw the bill, it showed 3 minutes on the phone with me and the other 17 spent on the phone talking with her?

Why is it that when a man knows that he has us where he desires us to be in our relationships that they just cannot seem to be satisfied with whom we are? My husband and I talked about many things that were bothering us in our relationship and we seemed to not have any problems communicating – but still something was causing him to try and keep a relationship with this other woman. He shared with me that she meant nothing to him, then why keep talking with her and sneaking behind my back keeping the conversation going? Was I a fool for telling myself that it was all right for him to talk to this other woman, I knew who he lived with, and whom he loved, but what did she mean to him? Should I care, or should I just let it go? My friends told me that I was stupid for letting this sort of behavior continue. What do you believe? Maybe one day you can drop me a line and share your thoughts with me. Maybe after enough of you inform me that I am a fool, I might just believe and move on; but for now it is not such a big deal.

Chapter Nine

Was I Stupid or Just Obedient to the Word?

Do you think that I was stupid for not caring about my husband really talking with the other woman? He told me she did not mean anything to him, and I wanted so much to believe this that I just put my thoughts on the Lord and asked Him to fix my husband. You see my friends I had became so content in the power of the Holy Spirit that I did not feel any discord or painful feelings when my husband continued talking to that other woman. Those had became his problems not mine, because you see I would not be held accountable for his sins, just my own. And I knowing that the Word says "that the wages of sin is death". I would not be the one held accountable at judgment day to be charged for his indiscretions, because I had enough of my own to be held responsible for already. And in knowing this, it was enough to keep my heart from being torn apart. In the word, the Bible lets us know that whatsoever we soweth, that is what we shall reap.

I stayed connected to the church and I attended services regularly and was being in constant communication with the Lord and fellowshipping with other Christians. We were receiving sound instruction and doctrine in the teachings of the Lord, and our Pastor and First Lady really believed in women honoring their husbands and husbands being committed to their wives. It was my belief that no matter what our husbands did, that our First Lady believed that their sins would end, and we would be all right as long as we stayed deeply committed to prayer; the Lord would bless our marriage and fix our husbands. Yet I was raised with a different set of rules, and those were still warring deep down in my soul. They went like this, if a man acted like a fool and stepped outside their marriage, you were to leave them. So I really had a huge battle going on deep within my Spirit, but the Lords words kept me content.

Therefore, I was not led to walk away from my marriage, because my desire to please the Lord and be saved carried more weight. It was worth more than rubies or diamonds. Anyway I had never actually caught him having an affair with another woman. Yet for some reason it always seemed to me as though I just should not trust any man. Why wouldn't those thoughts just slip away, was beyond my own comprehension. I guess truly it was just because I had such a tarnished relationship with the men of my past. The ones I believed I should have been able to trust most of my life, my father included. My real father had never done anything to harm me physically, yet unbeknown to him; I believed he never loved me either. He was never home with us; we were always left with our stepmother. He was out living his own life and she was home angry at the fact that she had to take care of his kids.

So, my husband really had his work cut out for him – in trying to get me to believe that he could be trusted, especially since I kept finding the number of another woman he has stayed connected to since our marriage. Whenever I brought up the fact that I was tired of him continuously talking with that woman, he told me it is not my business who he talked with. He always told me "as long as he was paying the bills I just needed to be quiet, "he said" "because you are not going to do nothing but talk". So I just keep pushing my feelings aside and acting as though it didn't really bother me, but it did.

Even today I believe at times I am really fed up with just letting him getting away with his actions, and even listening to my church Mothers who tell me to just give it to the Lord. At times I try to convince myself that the Lord does not desire us to be treated as doormats, and without respect. A marriage is supposed to be different than just a regular boy/girl relationship. When do we hold our men accountable for their actions?

I am going to share with you now through all that I have learned in teaching others about what ingredients goes into establishing healthy relationships, in looking at my own relationship with my husband. Many might say that I am stupid or crazy for putting up with his conversations with another woman, but who's to say that anything romantic was ever shared or discussed between them? Or even if it was, does that mean that they carried out any of their thoughts? I believe it could have been a possibility, but what I did not know could never spread discord!

Just because I am willing to deal with my husband talking to another woman on the phone does not mean you will decide to tolerate that sort of behavior in your relationships. But as an advocate, I will never tell you to leave your relationships that will always be your own decision to make. What I will always be willing to do is share with you resources in community that is available to you and/or your families and even some of the dynamics that goes into establishing healthy boundaries with your partner/mates that are different than some of the current tactics that I chose to utilize in my present relationship with my own husband. The Lord gave each of us minds to choose what we desire for our lives, you go out and learn all that you can about the ingredients that goes into building a strong relationship for yourselves; I am just an exchanger of information.

Chapter Ten

Teaching a New Style of Living

You see I teach self-esteem and healthy relationships trainings and all that I have learned while teaching these classes I kept close to the core of my very own existence. In studying up and finding sound instruction to share with so many women and children, I had to learn to walk the walk I was sharing. My goodness what difference knowledge makes in learning how to be led by sound doctrine, and then share that wisdom with others until it becomes the depth of who you are.

Each week I planned my lessons according to the outcomes of our previous classes, and I always based what was to be taught on some of the issues that came up in our classroom. You see what I found out from working with women who are facing multiple barriers is that we need to allow them to share current issues, so they would have help with learning how to cope with their situations. When you are raised without a lot of support it is really hard to determine a healthy way to address your barriers.

In educating those you work with it takes more than just telling them to read some resources that you might be willing to share with them. It would be the same for you or me, or even your children when giving them instruction. Sometimes it will take more of your time, I know than you believe you are responsible for sharing. But this is our jobs as mothers, educators, teachers etc.

If we are ever to have a better world for our children or selves to live in, then it is our responsibility to be willing to give all we can to make that difference. Yes I know some of the people we will come in contact with, just seem too stubborn to deal with, but what if their roles were reversed and it was you who desired help? How much would you believe you deserved the other person to put into sound instruction? If you can say to yourself that it would not matter how little the person was willing to put into making sure you got what was being taught, then I guess you have a right to feel like it does not take all that on your part either. But if your thoughts are that you deserved more than they gave, then I would give more of myself to make sure they got the best of what you knew to give!

Chapter Eleven

Learning Obedience to the Word

Since I had been stubborn all of my life when I joined Greater St. Paul Church of God in Christ, in Minneapolis it was hard for me to accept someone teaching me how to listen. You see I had met Mother Thomas quite a few times when I was out there in the world with my mini skirts and high heeled shoes. She would always invite me to attend their church and I would always inform her I was not ready to go that way. What I never had shared with her prior to coming to church is that she was slowly drawing me in to seek out the Lord, and I could not understand as to why she just would not give up on asking me that same question.

Much later on though it was out of my respect for her diligence in praying for my soul that I came to their church and in being there, I would sat in the back of the church and never came to the front as I cried deep within my heart as Pastor Thomas preached. What he did not know is that when he went over the scriptures they were convicting me of my previous sins. At the time that I was crying I had left the world as I had known it and was now living a different life. I had heeded to the word and was struggling for ways to keep living according to the straight and narrow path.

Every Sunday I was there in church and I was learning the word, not only from their teaching, but from reading it for myself. You see you have to try the word for yourselves, in order to really change the way we had lived our lives. The more I learned, the more I desired to eat more of the word. A real transformation was taking place in my life and I was learning to love the person that I was becoming.

I would seek out opportunities to share the words of the Lord with other friends of mine from my past and they did not desire to hear what I had to say. No longer was I looking for ways to get high because now I was high on life itself. My ways of living was no longer in vain, I could speak life giving words into someone's life, not those curse words that I had always found coming out of my mouth. The things I shared with my friends did not reel them in, they were still thinking of ways to get their next high. So I had to find a new set of friends, but I was not yet ready to give up all of my cute clothes for those that I saw the Mother's of our church wearing. Their way of dressing was still a turn off for me, but I so desired to be holy.

What we must learn for ourselves in trying to live a saintly life is that we must take our eyes off of other people, and live the best life we can and be free. Free from the hindrances of our past behaviors, because salvation I found out was independent of not only our mothers and fathers, but our children as well. No matter how much we desired our children to take on our new way of living, they had to decide individually what style of living was easiest for them to hold true to. At times I would find myself seeking from within how to share with them this new medicine I had grabbed hold of and kept close to my heart. Yet, it was not something that we could force feed and they would be able to digest it for a life changing transition.

Staying true to the word was more than a conversation to me, and I have had to daily eat more and more of what I had been taught, because I desire to make sure I get this right. I have found nothing worth allowing myself to be separated from the Lord, "for what is it to gain this whole world and lose our souls". I myself would count it all with voids. Life is as amazing as we allow it to be. That is if we can work on keeping our feet from slipping down slippery slopes. If we desire to be heavenly, let the spirit of peace reside within our hearts then nothing will be able to separate us from the love we have found in the Lord.

Many may have asked me how I have kept myself staying the course of the straight and narrow. I myself have had to share with many of them that it has not been through any power of my own. Because I never had this much sense before, and that I knew it was only His holy spirit that has done that for me.

Finally in closing this chapter off I will never put God on anyone, but I will say that for me, He has changed my perspective on which I was born to be! Live your best life my friends and do more right than wrong and that I promise will change your mindsets. Be your own encourager if you cannot touch your maker, be it what ever religion you have chosen for your self. I may not be able to touch mine, but I do know when I call upon His name, he enters my heart and life is as sweet as a candy bar.

Chapter Twelve

Rashon's Story

My son Rashon said to me after reading my book, *"Robbed of a Childhood, Raped by the System"* momma I am a little angry at you because you robbed me of my part in your book. I said what are you talking about honey, he said, you never shared with the world how bad I was, and I said honey I did not write my book to make you look bad, I wrote it so that the world might know my hidden pains. Then I said "Rashon" you were not a bad boy, you had a few issues, but you were still a wonderful son. I loved you then, and I love you even more today. Yet, he wanted to have his issues shared, so I am sharing this part of my son's life in hopes that it might help you with your struggles to be the best mom you can be.

When Rashon was in first grade society decided that my son did not fit in with the normal classroom structures and wanted him to be labeled as a child with Attention Deficit Disorder, with Hyper Activity. This was established by his teachers because he often got bored with their lessons. They would call me at home and ask me to come and pick him up, he loved being at home with me, and so this option soon wore thin on my nerves. So we had to try and figure out a new way for him to get his education and not be constantly pulled from the mainstream classroom structure. When this happens to our children they miss so much of their basic concepts.

Rashon was not a bad child; he was very inquisitive and had a very high I.Q. because he had been tested at the age of 6 years with an I.Q. level of 160. Therefore, he was bored with what was being shared with him during the normal classes he was within. When we would go to the stores Rashon would hide under the clothes racks or take off running really fast and end up in a separate isle. I would many times just start crying, really going frantic wondering if maybe someone might snatch him and I would loose him forever. But I would always find him before time to leave the stores. After a while these behaviors became very noticeable and I had to decide how to get past those issues. So after around three schools tried to get me to put him on Ritalin. I shared in my previous book that I had to ship him off to Indianapolis to my stepmother for awhile. Well she enrolled him in school and everything was going fine, and then one day they received his school records from Minnesota and the first thing they said is oh my God! We must put him on Ritalin or he is going to do something wrong here too.

Once my stepmother had him see a doctor and Ritalin was prescribed for him, it was not soon after Rashon started talking about Jason on Friday the Thirteenth. Momma became afraid and asked me to come and get him because he might just cut her head off while she was sleeping. Well I went and picked him up from Indiana and enrolled him back into mainstream classroom. It was not soon after that they started talking the same old things over again. I needed to go up to the school and pick him up and bring him home to be with me. Well one day someone shared with me information on one of the Centers that assist parents with their rights as they related to our children and their problems within the classroom. I was told that the school had to keep him in class until it was time for class to be over with. Then he would be my responsibility, well once Rashon was home he was acting out, kicking holes in the walls, throwing balls at his brothers' head. Things were at times really getting out of hand and I did not know what to do. So I was informed by his Psychiatrist that I had to enroll him in a special school that worked with children with behavior difficulties.

When I would go to visit him at this particular school, I never liked some of the comments I was hearing out of the mouth of the other children at the center. So I shared with several of the Counselors that my son had never used such words before. I once recalled being told that he shared with several of them (the women counselors) that they were $20 whores who could be found on one of Minnesota's main Streets. I asked where in the world you got those thoughts from Rashon, he shared with me that he had heard some of the other kids at the center saying that. Well I left him at the center a little longer and then one day I went to visit him and he was not in his room. I asked where my son was and they said in the quiet room, what quiet room I inquired. They took me to where he was rolled up in a mat and all I could see was his little head sticking out from the mat. I told them to remove my son from that mat and I was taking him home. And I never took him back to that school again.

You see my son was never without a brain, and was not a bad child. Schools that do not specialize in working with kids who have high IQ's do not always know how to figure out how to handle an overactive child, and therefore, at times categorize them as ADD/ADHD. And no I am not saying that teachers like labeling kids as bad who are not bad. But some teachers need more specialized training in order to determine some of the strengths and/or weaknesses of our children. There will also come a time when we might run into teachers who were not meant to be teachers. Some choose their professions because maybe their parents were teachers or thought being a teacher might be a good field of expertise for them.

I removed Rashon from that school for children with behavior difficulties his Psychiatrist told me it might be nice for Rashon to meet his real father. You see he had not known his real father, nor had he ever met him as far as I knew. Then one day I was talking to my babysitter's sister and she informed me that Rashon's dad had seen him when he was a little baby. So when he came to Minnesota and found her home and inquired as to where we were; she phoned my house where I was living with my husband and asked if he could come and meet his son. To make a long story short I allowed him to meet him and Rashon ended up in Texas where he eventually graduated with flying colors and had his choice of over 200 colleges.

Rashon visited five Colleges and ended up going to a College in Indiana for about a year, full scholarship for football. He then ended up being accepted at a College in Abilene, TX where he played football there for another year or so. Now he is building windmills all throughout Texas amongst other states. I am so very proud of my son and he is married with two beautiful children.

What if I had continued listening to the school he was in, and not taken him off Ritalin or even allowed him to have met his real father. Where would he be today? Mothers you need to know your children and their ways, and also believe in who they are from a mother's perspective. This way you will not allow the world to just label them any sort of way and be willing to accept their diagnosis as the only god there is, because sometimes it is good to ask questions.

I have always shared with Rashon, as well as my other children how very proud I am to have been blessed to be their mother. And I could not ever honor Rashon enough for the father/man that he turned out to be to his children and wife.

Chapter Thirteen

Inside a Mother's Heart

There is something I never shared with my kids since learning to be a domestic violence advocate. I found out that all families are different and we use the ingredients we had learned how to put together from our mothers and fathers. But if those mothers and fathers did not have it right within them we still had a distorted view of life, which in turn caused us to raise our children from an incomplete example. Where do we find the right tools to get this thing called parenting right? I for one believe it does not hurt to buy as many books as we can on appropriate parenting skills. Today there are so many resources out there that I never even knew existed. Why, because I thought I was living it right and found out through much experience as a hurt mother with a shattered lifestyle I was shattering you guys as well.

This is from my heart to yours, I am sorry I felt broken and torn between two worlds and that I allowed my shameful childhood memories to spill over into your lives, and since I felt "Robbed of a Childhood, Raped by the System". You probably felt and still feel the same way too! Right now and right here I am asking each of you to help me get this thing right before I leave this world. I am still hurting, but I am still functioning too! Are you trying to do both? Are we never talking, but yet still hurting, not only ourselves, but each other? Let's together stop this thing I have learned to call a generational curse. I do not desire my grandchildren to feel the pain we all still carry inside, why, because we don't have to allow this to go on this way. We can share our pains and the world can heal through our healing.

My precious daughter, I know because of the pain I continue to hide inside regarding my feelings of abandonment, even though momma died of cancer when I was just eleven years old. I carried the pains of her leaving and my not being ready to let go all of my life, and I feel in turn I have pushed you away for fear of your not accepting all of the choices I have made throughout my life with you and your brothers either. Just the other day I was having a conversation with my husband Tee and it was about my desires to try and get this thing called a relationship right between you and me, he asked me if maybe you felt abandoned by me? I started to try and share how I felt as things pertained to you in that particular situation and I broke down.

So I know I do feel that you may have some thoughts of my abandoning you when I left town to go to work. Yet I never learned then to take the time and explain to you where I was going, because I was ashamed of my work. Today I can tell you, I have never been ashamed of our love for one another. But we never took the time to get it right. Today honey I want to get it right with you too! Why, because I do not desire leaving this world without letting you know that I would die for your love and acceptance of who I am, just Mom.

To my first born son, Jesus, "my son", so much of our childhood memories were the same and I just found so many hidden hurts out! Things a mother would never desire to hear from a son's past, but we are so very strong inside our pains. We have been able to weather so many journeys together and you have always been a constant joy and the one I called my jokester! Yet, still I believe you too probably felt somewhat abandoned too when I was leaving town and allowing your father to keep all of you with him, and this is a special message from me to you, and that is if I could take any part of that time of separation back. I would do it in a heartbeat, but I can't, but there is one thing I can promise you and that is I will never abandon either of you ever again, that is until the day I die. And when that happens, it is my belief you all will have felt so loved that you will know I stayed as long as time allowed.

To my third son, we have some stuff going on between us, because I had to share with you a secret I carried until you were 30 years old. It was my secret to carry I believe because I did not desire you to wear the pain I bore. You see honey I believed no matter whether I had been raped and you were born out of that rape or not, my love for you would always be the same. To me a real mother did not look at how she was blessed to conceive you, she was grateful to the Lord that you had all of your fingers and toes. So many mothers could not share that blessing with their children or thank the Lord for that reward. Why, first of all some of them did not understand how to call out to Him, I did! You tell me that I held you back from sports as a child and if that is the way you feel to this day. I will accept this painful concept of where you are at in your heart as well, because I probably did not learn the best way to share that information with you before this point in my life either. What mother would want to cause her son the pain of knowing that he was born to her through being raped by her own first cousin? This for me was a very shameful situation, and I did not desire you to believe you were born out of shame. You were not, so until I could share with you I was not ashamed of myself I kept this quiet too!

I probably would not have even told you when I did except, Tee and I had heard comments coming down the line that someone other than myself was sharing this news to a portion of your world. It was at that time I decided to share the information with you, so it would not be as painful, and I guess there would never have been a good time to open this up to you! As my son all I can ask is that you do not hate me the rest of your life for what I believed would help you know how truly loved you are and will always be. My very special son and I will always be your only birth mother too!

Since allowing Rashon to go to Texas to meet his father my life has held a void. It was one of the hardest things I had ever had to deal with in my life. But as a mother you do what you believe is going to be best for your child/children. There has always been what seemed like a void in my life because of the distance between me and my son Rashon. But not only with him, with my other four children as well, yet they are all still here in Minnesota and if I desire to see them. The distance is not that far to travel, and therefore, I can just get in the car and drive to them without any hassle. With Rashon it would be all together different.

Also because of the way that I was raised as a child not really getting to be a child or learning how to be in a close knit family. I believe it has not allowed me to learn how to be close to my own children, and at times I still believe I could have used sounder instruction on how to be a better parent. Today I know that skills such as parenting has to be learned or taught and therefore, we as parents must make sure we learn all that we can, so we can transfer some of those skills onto our own children. Then they can share it with their kids as well.

To my last son the Lord allowed me to share my heartbeats with, what I want you to know is that when I divorced your father my second husband. My leaving you behind to live the whole school year with him and summers with me, I believed was the best thing I could have done, because I believed you would have obtained a better education out there than where I moved to. Today I believe since we were so very close all of us back then; that was probably not the right decision either. I say this because I feel a distance between us that I never felt as that child growing up! All throughout my life I kept making excuses to myself, saying I was doing what was best for my children. Never once did I believe I was doing what was best to keep my shameful lifestyle hidden. But today after being blessed to work with so many others whose past seems similar, I feel so many of us were broken. But it is time to stop this broken model and establish a new one. So son I am saying to you as all of your moms I want to get this thing called family right. Will you all give me the chance to change my wrongs and make them right? I love you all with an undying love, so I ask that you all teach me what you have learned about real love. And finally together we will get it right.

This is to my precious step daughter, whom I do not see as a step daughter, but one of my children. You see when we marry husbands who have children from previous relationships they too become our own. That is if we truly meant the vows we made, which consisted of till death do us part, and in sickness and in health. This to me means we are taking on the whole package and I want her to know that even though at times she might not believe I have this down pat, let us stay connected at the heart. Because I know that she knows that I love her too without conditions and I ask her to keep on allowing me to take up some space in her heart. We have been through some up times and some down times and that has been the same with all of our children.

Life is but a journey and even though we are all dealt a particular set of cards, it is up to us to choose which ones to play throughout our lives. So many times during my trainings I had shared how I made it through many of the trials and tribulations I was faced with. It has not been easy to accomplish all the things that I have been blessed to achieve. And yes there have been times that I wanted to just throw my hands up in the air and give up. That for me was not an option I chose to take, because that would have meant that I had little faith. The Bible taught me that if we had little faith we would never be able to move those mountains that was placed before us. How could we have expected to be winners in this game called life if we were never willing to go through the pain it took to change?

You see my friends we all have been through something, and my question to you is how did you come out at the end of your test? Did you see yourselves as winners or losers? Would you be willing to share your brokenness so readily and be open for judgment as I am placing myself before you? Or would you be one of those who would have said it does not take all of that to be free? If you were, then you too, are still holding on to some baggage you need to rid yourself of; so that you can move on past stagnation to freedom. When you take the time to taste what real freedom is like, you will never go back and make those same mistakes that kept you stuck previously again.

Chapter Fourteen

How Do I Truly Share With You What It Has Been Like?

This journey of mine has not been an easy one, especially living day to day trying to figure out how to get life right when you had lived it so wrong previously. It was not going to be an easy thing to accomplish and this is something I knew from my core, but I knew that it would be necessary to become someone I was never allowed to be and that was Mary. The majority of the life I had remembered living was always giving my power over and finding my strength inside someone else. To have done what they desired of me, but never what I desired to do for myself. How did I begin to count up new ways of adding value to being me, when there had never been a real individual "me" in sight? If I was not figuring out how to take care of my children, I was serving the men in my life, so I had no time to be free.

After leaving my job from one of the major non-profits in Minnesota I decided because of the experience of working as an intermediary, meaning "one not directly responsible" for providing services to the so called "hard to place populations". It was my passion to be a direct service provider, but I had no experience. So the first thing I had to do was learn how to provide re-entry services to those women, men and youth exiting corrections. I did this by signing up for every training focused in those areas, so I became well educated/versed in mediation, circle training/keeper, victim offender dialogues, methadone treatment techniques, and a committed domestic violence advocate/leader in this community and throughout Minnesota.

I did not only desire to learn it, I had to find forums and jobs where I could practice what I had learned. My passion grew in the areas of being a direct service provider. But remember I had created a not-for-profit organization and I had to establish a board of directors, establish a funding base, and learn how to run this organization all aspects of being a leader. So one of my very first grants that I had went after turned me down, then I tried again for that same grant the next year and again I was turned down. By the time the third year came around for their funding I said I was not going to apply for it, and my board convinced me to try one more time. Well to make a long story short we received the funding. It was for a $10,000 Capacity Building grant and this meant me and/or several of my board members could go through yearlong leadership development training.

No one on the board was able to go through the workshops because most of them had full time jobs themselves. So not only did I have to figure out how to obtain more funding to do the work I believed I was called to do, I had to find time to go to the workshops every Tuesday for a year. They were being given through one of the Colleges here in Minnesota and if I had, already had my B.A. at the end of the training I would have earned my MBA in Business. As you might well imagine to date I still have not found the time to earn my B.A. Yet I did not allow that to discourage me and when I had completed those training sessions out of 33 organizations that had been chosen to receive the funding. I was chosen by the grantor to be highlighted in their National E-Newsletter as the leader more apt to go to the next level. This made me believe that now we were on our way to the next level of management.

I worked on writing another grant and this one was for our first fundraiser and we asked for $2,500 and were awarded our second grant. It may have been small but it made our hearts large. Here I was once again so happy for such a wonderful accomplishment, but I did not know the first thing about fundraising and so I took most of the money and brought food, napkins, plates, forks, spoons etc. We decorated the place we held the fundraiser. Everything we used for the fundraiser we purchased with the money we got from the grant. We even brought a computer at a discounted rate to raffle off to raise more money. I took it on myself to cook enough food for up to one hundred people. For a while I began to believe that I had never worked so hard in my life. My board members all helped to decorate the room; we all helped serve around 50 people who attended our first fundraiser. They shared with all those in attendance why they chose to work with me, I cried, because they made me feel so very proud of our work, and even though we did not make a profit. The room was filled with love and appreciation from those in attendance and it was shared through their open-ended comments and gratitude.

We were on a roll and so I wrote our third grant and we received $9,000 to have a strategic action plan established to guide our organization to its next level of operation. I was surprised that we had to pay a planner most of the $9,000 grant just for a day and a half worth of work; thinking my goodness. How in the world does anyone earn that kind of pay just for taking down thoughts we already had been putting into operation and make it sound good on paper, it was our thoughts after everything was said and done that the proposed scope of work was not enough to take us to where we desired to go. Yet, I did not believe we still knew enough to pull the next steps of operation off, and neither did our board. So we felt somewhat stuck; not knowing what to do next.

After about 3 years going by with us coming together on a continuous basis, my board of directors asked me to start going after contracts so that I might get paid for all the meetings and free trainings that I had been doing. I believed that was just part of my job for trying to establish a business, whether I was being paid or not. They did not agree with my thoughts and my commitment, and I was glad that they did not, because my husband and I would probably be homeless ourselves as well. But that still was not enough to deter me from being committed to bringing about changes within the lives of as many men, women and youth that the Lord would bless me to come into contact with. It would not stop me from volunteering to do circles of supports within the schools for young men who many times some believed no matter what we did, would not change their self-destructive patterns of living.

The work we did in community schools did prove them to be wrong as we watched some of the young men graduating from those classes, classes they said did not teach them as much as we were teaching them in our circles of support. We did not make up the words for them to exchange with us, they did this on their own accord and without any prompting on our own behalf! We sometimes say life is a trip and then we die, well I say life is all that we put into it, and why not try to bring about change for as many lives as we can? You see, someone a long time ago invested some time into helping me change the path I once traveled, and because of that I will continue giving back to society as much as is humanly possible. My work is not based upon pay, even though we all need it to pay our own bills. The Lord has continuously made a way for us to scrimp by and manage to get by, and for the moment that is enough.

Chapter Fifteen

The Day I Asked for a Raise

One day I entered the office of one of the Director's I was working under contract with and I approached her and said I needed a favor. She said what can I do for you, I said I need a raise and that it had been three years that I had been under contract with her, never asking for a raise. My workload had increased and the efforts I put into creating curriculum were taking me four and one half hours to finish. Yet, at the end of it all I was only being paid for the direct services I was supplying. So two hours and thirty minutes of my time was just like making a donation to the program. It was at that time that Ms. Ruby agreed with me that my work was worth more than I was being paid, but since she had went after a certain amount of money during her RFP process - until that grant is lived out you have no extra funds to pay out. What she said to me is that your contract will remain the same until 2011 and even though we love your work, I cannot give you more pay, but we will help you out in other ways to make this a better option for you, and so I left her office feeling reassured.

You see everyone for me it was not just about the pay, it was about a program that I knew was working better than any program I had been blessed to be a part of, and I knew that she and her whole staff cared about the outcomes of these women's lives. That to me was worth more than its weight in gold. You see what Ms. Ruby never knew was that I was more grateful to her than she had personally hear coming from my mouth.

What I have learned over these years of being out there on the front lines trying to establish partnerships/contracts is that not many people were willing to take you under their wings and give you a chance. When you share with leaders that you were willing to work with the people so hard that you might work yourself out of a job this frightened them too, who wanted to lose their jobs? Not many I ever recalled running into. But what I would share with anyone is that just because we teach the people we were blessed to serve how to navigate through systems for themselves, would not hinder their chances of working with new participants/clients.

Many still found that it would be easier to work with those they knew something about than to continue bringing in a stream of new program participants. If you were an employer and it was your responsibility to hire committed employees, who would you have kept on staff? Would it have been worth your time and the extra expense it took to train in a new employee, or would you have preferred keeping those you already was comfortable with? We all might have chosen the latter, but my heart was committed to what many called the underdogs. My reason being, I was once considered one of those people too, and depending upon who you would ask; I am still one of those people. But others tell me today, that I earned my stripes to be at the top level. A level of growth to me was just going through the process, ask the ladies I serve we go through the same process together. That is what makes the difference in the way some of us do our work.

As a new and upcoming leader in our community, I did not understand those dynamics of the business, but all of us have a different focus and passion. Maybe that is what happens after you have been in the business for a specific amount of time. My prayer was that I hoped that I would never have to get like some in order to continue doing the work I so richly desire to do.

Chapter Sixteen

No One Informed Us It Would Be So Hard

The next steps I worked to establish was building relationships with other organizations throughout our community so that they would know our passion, our desires to provide re-entry services to men, women and youth exiting corrections. So I met up with several of the people I had went through the year long leadership development trainings with and they called me in to do a presentation to their group, and I did. After the presentation they had an article placed about that presentation on their National Website. It was a wonderful write-up and it opened the door for me to go out and do other presentations throughout our State. So many calls were coming in from those inside corrections because I was volunteering to go into the prisons and do job fairs or transition fairs that Corrections sponsored.

Now we were being seen as the organization to provide employment services to those exiting corrections, but what no one has known is that I have never turned anyone of those callers down. I have provided resources to them in record numbers for no pay what so ever. Why, many would ask me and my only answer was, is that once someone offered me a little free advice and it changed my life. It cost none of us anything to be kind to someone.

As time passed by, I was beginning to become a little discouraged, but one thing that always kept me going was my faith in the Lord. He was the only one that I knew to call on at all times that have never let me down. The world, might let us down, our children might let us down, family might let us down, friends might even let us down, but the Lord is always there for you; and He is always on time.

One thing I teach all the women, men and youth I work with is a great attitude will take them to places they would never reach if they had a bad one. I will never tell you that you will not accomplish your goals if you try hard enough. But one thing I will make sure I share with you and that is, it is not what we know, it is who we know in this state that takes you to the next level.

It is up to you not to let your hearts be troubled by the conditions of this world, or by the way the people of this world treat you, and whatever you put into life, always comes back to you. You are to be encouraged, be blessed, knowing that you and only you hold the keys to your outcomes.

We are now faced with the reality of the great recession of 2009 and I do believe that almost every charity is under more pressure to come up with more of their own innovative solutions to reach a broader demand for resources. And I like everyone else is faced with a more challenging environment and we have to do more for less.

Chapter Seventeen

The World That Believed We Were Not Worth Much

For years I have worked to try and bring about change in the lives of those I have been blessed to serve. I volunteered for one organization for over nine years as a domestic violence public educator/speaker, working to spread the word of how violence affects our communities, families and the world at large. No one ever was asked to pay me a dime for the work I did, but you can believe those organizations were raising large amounts of money. I often wondered why there were not more advocates being created from the very people they were serving. That was until the day I decided to create my own organization and help the men, women and youth I met in the world to truly transform their lives.

You see people love to pity those of us whom they deem unfortunate and who might have had a raw deal growing up, but when you desire to seek their help in creating your own organization because you believe if you work hard and share your experiences the participants you worked with would learn to advocate for themselves and navigate through systems in ways they had never known before. This way we would have been working ourselves out of jobs and being put in a position to create something new, but the world is not looking to work themselves out of their jobs. They like giving us little bits and pieces of the puzzle. That way we will always be needy and they will always have a job saving us poor people. I began to pray that the Lord keep me poor in thought, but not allow us to become commodities, because we should not be seen as anyone's meal tickets, we were supposed to be the ones being taught ways of stabilizing our own lives to find new ways of living beyond existence. Life was meant to be lived and not dangling on the end of the ropes you give us and tell us we had to cope with whatever you put before us.

Back when Welfare was an option our bills could only be so much, we could only make so much or we would be cut off and do not become too educated then we were a threat to your very livelihood. Your paychecks, even those whom I had volunteered for and had helped build their businesses would not help me to build my business. They believed the very people I served would desire to be my program candidate rather than theirs. I wonder why? Could it have been because they were learning how to love themselves and that they did not have to be helpless, isn't that what you were supposed to be teaching them/us?

Who are you to call yourselves advocates who bring about change, change in what? Your own ways of serving those in need and keeping us begging for crumbs. Isn't it true that even your dogs are allowed to eat the crumbs from underneath the table? We are not your dogs, or your puppets, but we are human beings just like you and we desire to raise our own children, to feed and clothe them as well. There is no way we desired to be treated like victims, but that is what the systems are structured to make us feel like.

It was my belief that slavery ended a long time ago? But in this world the way it has been structured for us to fit inside of – there is no room for growth within many of the programs you have designed to save the people. For our people suffer due to a lack of knowledge, because in your programming we were not pressed to get an understanding as to who and how the systems were structured. If we had read about urban sprawl, gentrification, or what all happens during a Caucus, my how much more we would have learned. It is time for change and change must come from within our own lives. We as a people have gotten too comfortable with taking the crumbs that have been rationed out to us, that we truly have forgotten how to fight for that which is rightfully ours.

I have decided that I will no longer just settle for the little bits and pieces people are willing to hand out to me when I am the one that is truly on the front line doing all or most of the work. I have been a volunteer in so many programs and none of those whose programs I have helped to save even tried to help me even a little bit. In Tennessee I was raised to believe we do unto others as we would have them do unto us, and just hope for the best outcome. Yet, in today's world not many are equipped to feel the same way. It is a constant take; take all you can from the little ones. What difference does it make anyway, who cares what happens to them, especially not as long as you accomplish your purpose, right?

Chapter Eighteen

How Do You Keep Going Against All Odds?

You keep going because you know if you don't, there is not going to be anyone else who will care more about your well being that you do. They ask me how do you keep going when, they believed there was no reason to and I would share with them that they were responsible for encouraging themselves. How do we encourage ourselves. You pick up a good book and read it, you read your Bible, you find some affirmations and you read them until they become a part of who you believe you were meant to be. These are some of the ways to be inspired to do something different with your lives. There is always hope, you just have to know within yourself that you deserve the best treatment there is and only you are responsible for the feelings you hold close to your chest. I have never recalled having anyone else inside my body making me do or say anything I was not willing to allow to come out of my mouth.

One of the Mothers from my church once shared with me that "out of the abundance of my heart, my mouth speaketh", when she shared that scripture with me, I was not pleased to hear those words being mentioned. It sort of made me angry at her, and she had not done anything to me. What I will share with you is that the understanding of that Scripture did not fully become clear until much later on in my journey. This new walk that I am living is a daily lesson, and if we are willing to submit ourselves and take the charges that comes with the offences; we will win this battle.

You see my friends what I learned about letting our lives be led outside our natural feelings is not easy, because we are in a constant battle of trying to keep our old behaviors, because they were comfortable to us. The new ways you desire to live, means that change must come and it is hard to give in to change, or at least, it takes courage, determination and effort. Even if you feel a struggle to do what is comfortable, resist that temptation and try what that little silent voice is prompting you to do. I promise you will not be sorry; you listened to those voices, coming from inside your core.

Chapter Nineteen

They Called Me Ms. Whitney

During a lot of my trainings the ladies would call me Ms. Whitney and it would make me feel so old and ancient. But if you can call me Ms. Whitney, it will make it easier for you to call your boss Mr. So in So, or Ms. So in So. You see ladies and gentlemen we are what we give over to practice, and without practice we will never become perfected in anything. Whom do you serve in this life you are living? Can you put your faith in something outside yourself? Isn't it worth thinking about, even if you cannot live it out? What about the children, who will be there for them if we do not go through something. I chose not to do drugs, smoke cigarettes purposely, because I believed it would better their odds of not picking up my bad habits.

My past lifestyle was no longer a present option for me, so each and every day I had to find something new that would drive me to a better outcome. If you do not plan to have a life you will just go through life existing. Living to exist is far less valuable than, existing to live. If you desire to be depressed, I promise you will get just what you are expecting. And I also promise you if you feel motivated, inspired, moved to change, you will bring that into existence as well. You see we call that into existence which we so readily think on.

What do you desire? Do you desire life, or do you desire death? Which ever you are seeking is just waiting at your door to come into your life, and manifest itself as your reality.

Chapter Twenty

It's a New Day

The time has come for all of us adults to come to the aid of those less fortunate than we ourselves have been. It is time for a new beginning and for us to share all the knowledge that we have acquired with those we have been serving as we teach them to go to the next level. Life is what we put into the creation of it, as Jesus spoke His words of life into existence, life became real and it grew into something amazing. Your words can speak life or they can speak death not only into the lives of our children, but all those who matter most to us. Mothers you must teach your children to not only love you, but to love themselves as well. Instill in them that they can be whatsoever they desire to be, and show them how to take a step by step process to getting there. When I was coming up I was never taught to be all that I could be, we were taught to work our butts off and then one day someone would acknowledge the great work we were doing and hire us, or give us a raise for a job well done. We were never told that we could be the builders or the designers of something great and wonderful.

How come we did not believe that we could be the President of our Country? Or the Mayor of our City was it because of the color of our skin? Why should skin tone determine our destinies? It shouldn't, but we have been so conditioned to believe that we are nothing and would never be anything, no matter how hard we tried.

For years I have worked not only to better the condition of my own thoughts, but to make way for a better life for my children. A legacy to leave behind that they can model their lives after, and then their children and their children's children, but is this really a possibility for them; or am I just believing in a pipe dream?

For someone such as myself, who has not only built two organizations from the ground up; but one who has continuously used their own contractual monies to establish and create the lessons I choose to teach the men, women and youth I have been blessed to teach/train. I never really liked having someone put any of us into a box and believe we all function at the same capacity because of lessons learned. It has always been my own belief that we are all individuals and we learn at different levels and speeds and that is all right too! Those designed cookie cutter approaches, has never really worked well for any one community of people.

What I found to be the best approach was to first of all go in and assess the situations of any given group of individuals and then make our determinations from what our findings bring about through our assessments. Each of us is on a journey and will come to terms with our state of being at our own levels of understandings and that is really all right. That is just the way the Lord designed each of us to be and be able to operate from that mode of comprehension.

Chapter Twenty One

Just Because I Believed Things Would Change

You see just because I believed that things would change because I was a self-starter, motivator and designer of programs and instructions did not mean that the world was going to embrace me, or even see me as a changed person. No one said just because I desired to clean up my life and live a new lifestyle that the world was going to allow me to do the same, or even be this newly designed creature! I found my self running into obstacles at every turn, and no matter how many lessons or classes I took I could not get many people to give me a chance to prove my capacity to deliver services.

I took every re-entry related classes that I could enroll in, and no matter what the cost was or who were putting on the workshops. I would call and ask if I could be awarded a scholarship. Many times the instructors would say to me, to just write a short statement as to why I desired to enroll in the training and what I hoped to accomplish from my new found knowledge. This for me was very easy, because the passion that was burning inside of me could easily be described.

Some of the other things I found myself doing were volunteering to be a domestic violence advocate, to perform workshops at many of the Colleges on a free of charge basis. This I knew would give me the exposure I needed to prove that I had a gift and I wanted to share my knowledge with the world, by providing direct services to many whom the world sometimes forgot about.

I even became a volunteer for one of the Conflict Centers in Minnesota who provided mediation services to community members, schools and a lot of other organizations throughout Minnesota. This was a huge commitment, but I found myself up for the challenge and the more I challenged myself to learn. The More I was capable to dealing with a lot of the different moods and changes the participants I was blessed to work with showed me! On a day to day basis, I would seek out different workshops that would enhance my capacity to deliver services to populations many considered hard to place. But no matter how much I learned, or how much experience I had, the world seemed to shy away from me and seemed to be afraid of the way I believed services should be shared.

You see when people become a commodity, a way of being a source of income that pays many an individual and groups salaries. People seem to loose their real value, and I never seemed to understand the hidden agendas; many of whom were working with this population seemed to have. I am not saying that people should not have jobs, but what I am saying is that we should sometimes work ourselves out of a job if we continue warehousing our own people to make a dollar. Bare with me for a moment, because you see I was once that individual many said would never be nothing, or amount to much, but today I believe I amount to quite a bit of experience and giving back to our community.

As a matter of fact in 2008, I earned the Jonathan Farmer Illuq Award for an exemplary Community Service Provider, and in 2010 I received the Governor's Faith Based and Best Practice and Community Service Initiative Award, the Spirit of Peace Award from one of the Conflict Resolution Centers I volunteer with and finally I also received the President's Lifetime Achievement Award for my many hours of community service. So I do not have a problem working to make a major difference not only in the person I once was, but as a person who believes in working to make amends for my mistakes and wrongs in my past life. In all that I have learned and worked to accomplish, I have never forgotten that I did not see myself as a worthy person. When you have low self-esteem it is pretty hard to esteem oneself on high, or even believe in one's own ability to make a difference in the life of others.

There had came a point in my life that I had to decide for myself that I did not want my children looking down on me in a casket saying my mother was not a good mother. Or a woman who put her own desires before seeking to care for them. Whether they were now adults or not, I was still their mother and because of that, I had a responsibility to act accordingly.

Chapter Twenty Two

Life Is Truly a Journey

It is one that I have learned that we can design the way we would like to have it turn out. So much of the old person that I was has been shed off, and a new creature appeared. Not only in the outside appearance, but I had to learn how to ask the Lord to help me shed all the ugliness that I had buried within the core of my very being. To ask Him to do away with all of my scarlet colored sins and cleanse me as white as snow, you see He said that He would do that for us; if only we would allow it to happen. This did not come without a willingness to be changed, and to begin to embrace change as something I could welcome.

You see none of us desire to be in pain, or to even believe that we deserve to be treated as though we were some sort of monster. Or a person not deserving of forgiveness, but the Bible that I found myself becoming more and more determined to live by, said "He Who Is without Sin" "Let Him Be The One To Cast The First Stone" and none decided to be the first to do that! So I believe I can rest my case. We have all sinned and fail short of the highest calling in our Lord and Savior Jesus Christ. Even if you do not believe in Jesus, you believe in something that is bigger than yourself, do you not?

I began to see life as a journey, one that I could partake of and be glad each day for something.

Even if my day was not designed or filled with the sort of ingredients that I would have filled it with, if I had established it! You see, life can be so full of our greatest expectations, or it can be filled with our largest downfalls. But I have learned that I am going to do all that I can to have my best day each and every day. What do you desire to establish for your own lives? We only live once and, why not just make the most of what we have?

I found out a long time ago that if I were to die, and my children were at my funeral, what would be some of the things I would want them to speak about most from the way I lived my life. And what I found out is that I did not desire none of my early years of living to be a part of their eulogy being told. Therefore, what that meant to me was that I had to do all that I could to change the course of my own life. So I ask all of you to not judge me by my past ignorance and stupidity, but by the content of my character that I have portrayed before you.

Chapter Twenty Three

The Rewards of Moving Forward

What has really kept me going forward was my faith in the Lord and how He had changed my imaginary thoughts of who I was and what I looked like. You see I found out that no matter how the world perceived me, or thought what sort of person I was being. At the end of all our journeys the Lord would make the final decision as to where I was going. And yes I know that Jesus is not the only spiritual father we serve. But I always shared all whom I was blessed to share my thoughts about our Savior with; they all knew for me I believed it was Jesus, always believing that faith was the substance of things hoped for and the evidence of things unseen. Those very words worked for me, especially at a time when I saw no hope in much else.

As I read more and more Scriptures I started learning what it meant to stay in the word and asking for spiritual guidance from some of my church Elders. I learned a lot about what standing on the Word of the Lord called me into being. I began to learn how to seek more knowledge and I began planning out my days of continuous education. Knowing that I desired something more than what once was my life and an attitude of gratitude. Because I learned that when you have felt harmed all of your life whenever you had another major accomplishment you wanted to share those accomplishments with the world. But I found out very quickly that just because I had became proud of what I was learning, did not mean that my new circle of friends whom I had previously helped was feeling the same way about me and those new found accomplishments. What I mean by this is that I would always shoot out an e-mail to that list of people I knew and not many would acknowledge the receipt of my message, there was hardly ever a time that they would even pick up the phone and say congratulations Mary you did an awesome thing.

You see I hoped that they would say, wow Mary that is really great or special. Because you see my friends I needed to be validated so I could feel I mattered, and this was what I wanted all those I served to know and feel. Because when I congratulated others for their accomplishments many would share with me their worlds grew. I found myself desiring my friend to love me enough so I would matter to them that way as well!

Now I am going to share with those of you who might have some of the same or similar thoughts as I once did. Do not set yourselves up for failure, or seek to find your validation inside someone else's thoughts, and you will truly grow to another level from within on your very own. And when this happens you will see another side of tomorrow that you can begin embracing even before the morning comes and shows you the light of day.

I have learned so very much, even though it did not happen that way for me because I do not desire for you to withdraw from society or your own growth. Don't allow your thoughts to say, "See Mary", no one really cares about you and who you are trying to become. Because it might just cause you to stop desiring to grow and just keep on working your butt off for yourself not because you are trying to prove to the world that you do have value or worth?

Another light bulb that had went off within me as I trained the men, women and youth in community is that I had never learned how to truly connect in the appropriate way with the world of business, because to me they were all about technicalities and I was all about the emotions. And when we allow our emotions to get in the way of our progress it stunts our growth, and our emotions would not draw in funding dollars.

My main goal in life was to instill worth and meaning into the lives of the most vulnerable populations, because I had learned through the process of self-examination that once those seeds of hope came alive self-worth became very relevant, but was irrelevant in the world of business. And I had to learn how to begin separating the two, if ever I was to draw funding into our program design and structure.

There were so many business professionals that I had helped move their projects ahead to the next level of their program operations. Because I understood "those people" they served, and what I never really understood is why they did not see themselves just as we all are; and that is "those people". Let any of us loose our jobs or positions and we will really see who "those people" are! But within their own minds they are not ever going to be a broken model like some of us. I was just considered a self made manager who was still seen as just an ex-working woman to many of them.

You see they would use me for my thoughts and dreams for implementing a new design for their program structures. But most times they would not give me a contract to do the work or allow me an opportunity to be written into a grant as a small partner with them either. They desired to keep all the funding in house for their own viability. I also found out in Minnesota this is what happens a lot of times to a lot of us small and upcoming organizations.

I believe especially when it came to me being offered a chance to prove my experience was beyond just passion, I would be cut off at the entrance. You see I had made it a point over these last six years since desiring to do the work I do to take every training/workshop I could find in the area of re-entry and conflict resolution skills. I did not just want to do the work because I had a passion burning within; I wanted to do it because my expertise had been obtained in the field. And my crushing past lifestyle made me the perfect advocate to be able to make the heart to heart connection with the women, men and youth I worked with.

Most times after obtaining the certifications, and classroom hours they would still bring in a person with a degree to deliver the services, while trying to give them some of my reflected designs. Once again I would be left with my passions to bring about change in the lives of "those people" because I felt not only did I have a passion to go deeper. I was still one of "those people" and I knew how to get to the core of their pains, because to me many times the pains they felt, most times I was feeling some of those same pains too! And what I truly never could put my fingers on was if they really desired those individuals to get better, why they would not allow someone such as me who had sought diligently to do this work, to do it with them!

Chapter Twenty Four

It Really Does Not Matter What They Believe

When the Lord showed me that it really does not matter what they believe as long as I am living all that I know to be a better person, living His word is what it takes to get to heaven. I was truly satisfied within my soul, and knew I would never turn back to my old behaviors. For it is at the end of our journeys He is the only one that will judge our works. We are not saved by our works any ways, but by the faith in our Lord and Savior Jesus Christ. That is all that really matters to me and I stay focused on the word, and no my old friends are no longer a part of my life, but I had to find new ones; who lived by some of the same standards that now guides my life.

I had never been one who allowed herself to get tangled up with many people and if I have found one or two great friends, then I am ahead of many out there in the world. So much fear from past hurts always seemed to appear within my thoughts, always believing that if I allow myself to trust. Then they too, would eventually harm me in some way. This sort of thought pattern might limit my circle of friends, but that is all right too!

I tried so many times to do work for many organizations to prove the value of the work I believe the Lord had called me to do and most of them would let me work with their program participants and/or clients. But when those same clients desired to purchase my book or support my work, it was hardly ever allowed. Once one of the organizations I worked with had one of their drivers bring a van load of the ladies to one of my book signings and allowed them to purchase my book. But I worked for that organization under contract for years and the fee I charged them to do the work did not even pay for the curriculum I created and printed out. Yet it was not about those in charge but the very women I served, so that they might see the Lord through the love and care I showed them. Then in turn change their own lives and discover the rewards of a real transformation which would be the light of a new way for their children/families to model their own standards after.

You see when we were in school we never had anyone teach us the value of high self-esteem and when you had grown up within a household where your parents fought and degraded one another. Our standards were not at the level they should have been at either. So you could only transfer to your children the value you had hid within your own core and it was accepted as truth.

Today I ask you to challenge your own truths and create for yourselves a new way of living and begin to live out that creation. For in the beginning of the world "Was the Word and The Word Was With God and the Word Was God". For years I studied what those words in Scripture meant and to my own conclusion I believed it meant. That we could establish within our thoughts a newly designed way of living and it would come into being. So I began to practice what I read and it seemed to come to life for me too! Therefore, I ask you to do the same in your own life and see what your outcome will be, it is worth the chance don't you think?

The reason I worked to that capacity is because so many years prior the Lord saw fit to forgive a host of sins I had committed against not only Him, but to oneself. It was my belief and is still my belief today, that if we live His words they, truly come to life within our own families. Our children then see a better future for themselves and we have become that more appropriate example. We must continue to demonstrate for them a certain set of higher standards and their outcomes will be better as well. I would always ask the Lord, why did I not understand His words previously as I do today, and I believe that we cannot question what was, but live what is today. And if the world does not give back to you, that which you have freely shared or volunteered with them do not get angry; just get busy. Do something for yourselves, and you will not be as dependent upon someone else's crumbs abilities to do it for us!

There are so many things that I learned to accomplish by utilizing my own learned abilities, things my stepmother said I would never be capable of doing. It was my own ignorance for believing her word was god. It was not, and today I know that through much experience and having had a desire to learn. I have learned that we get back out of this world that which we are willing to be taught and given through the prompting of the Holy Spirit. The Lord helps those who desire to help themselves. Each of us was born with God given talents, once put into operation creates so many new avenues for us to have a complete life giving experience.

You be blessed, be encouraged and do all that you can to accomplish your goals, but in order to do so you must establish some to dream or visualize and they then become your reality.

Chapter Twenty Five

When My Eyes Became Opened

I must finally share with the world that I really had to take my eyes, heart and thoughts off of other people helping me to get to the next level. It was not about them, and I did not have to please them, I had to learn how to love my inner self. This was not done without much letting go and allowing the naked word of the Lord to grow deep within my heart. It is not of this world that our thoughts are supposed to come from, for we may live in this current world, but we are not of this world.

The Lord had adorned me with His way of thinking and it was a humbling experience, one that I was truly not just sliding into accepting. My son Rashon even told me one day that he did not desire to speak with his saved mom. He wanted to speak to his old mom, the one that cursed all the time. Why, because he was angry and needed to vent and at the time I seemed just too nice and understanding. I was also using language that was not easily accepted by him at the moment either. I informed him that my old way of being no longer took precedence over my life, and whom he was speaking to at the moment was my new way of living. Even though it hurt and I wanted to reach out and satisfy his whimpering I could not allow myself to allow my fleshly ways to sneak its ugly face back into my thoughts.

I have also found that it appears that the world could hold me better if I could just let certain words just roll off the tip of my tainted tongue. There were even times when I would try and figure out whom I could call that would be willing to let me talk about where the Lord had delivered me from. It was not a large network of friends who was excited about hearing from me or having me even dials their numbers. But no matter what, I still had to keep on pushing on and seeking the word of the Lord. Because the more you study, the more able we are to arrive in a space in our lives where the Lord would always have His holy spirit in operation.

I believed and had been taught over these last 14 years that we must be on a continuous quest for quality improvement of ourselves, and it only comes from staying in fellowship with other saints and those seeking the undivided word of our living God and Savior Jesus Christ. Some of my friends would at times say I must believe now that I am better than them and I would have to just let those words roll off my back. Then I would have to share with them that just was not the way I felt, but I did feel that I could no longer allow their ways to be my ways. I could not even go to a bar, smoke drugs, or cigarettes for fear of allowing old behaviors to creep back into my life.

My life today has kept me inside my home more than I have been out socializing in the world at large. But my thoughts have been cleaner, my life has been fulfilling in many ways, and no it has not been what I believed is a perfect life. But it has been so much sweeter than the past life I had led.

In order to stay on the straight and narrow I have had to change not only my past behaviors, but the way I believe people should act towards me, as well as the way I allow my thoughts to take hold of me. We are beyond our thoughts and we can accomplish anything we desire to allow this universe to bring back to us. Because we get most times that which we are willing to allow to come back to us, even if it is anger, resentment, hatred or even jealousy; which is as cruel as the grave.

Finally in closing I thank the Lord for those few friends of mine that has stood by my side, especially Susie Hodges even when I did not have a realistic view of life. I knew that my thoughts were distorted at times and I could not always see their side of things, but I did not understand how to really explain my internal pains to them in depth either. Yet I could always be a little bit more open with Susie about some of my most hidden fears and I always loved the way she treated me as a friend. One day I remember she said Mary you are just going to have to try and trust someone. So I allowed myself to open the gap a little bit more and as we took more baby steps I believe I trust her more than I have any other person in my life for some time. We will just continuously stand in the gap for each other and that too is all right.

To my children and my husband who truly make up my best world. I am so very glad to have had them in my life and I would not trade either of them for different models. For they are the best that the world has to offer and a heartfelt thanks to my children and husband, Aunt Mary, Ada Gill, Mother Garrett, Susie Hodges, my father Bennie Brown, my brother Bennie R. Brown, my sisters Tracy and Lisa Brown, Jimmie L. Coulthard, Guy Gambill, Stephen and Sara Galligan, the Whitney family, Hattie Bonds, Mary Paradis for Mr. Arte Cunningham, Bill Bundy and many Spiritual friends whom I will not call by name for fear of missing to mention someone important for standing by my side. What many of them do not know is that the world is brighter and much fresher than it ever has been before.

This is to "those people" who each day allowed themselves to take the sharing of our flaws to another level. A level even the world could not hear was possible inside our frailties. You gave me so much time in your lives and I thank you from the bottom of my heart, because I found room to breathe inside our sharing and I pray you will continuously grow and enrich the lives of your families through your own growth and now expertise in the field of healing.

We are tomorrow's dreams of a better world for all of us, especially our children, but I ask that you do not dream small any longer and that your dreams stretch as far as the mind could imagine. If there was one thing I learned in this world we live in today and that is that many of us place ourselves in those small boxes.

You be blessed, be encouraged and know that we have to give ourselves permission to feel valued and know that our work within those organizations made way for a new way of delivering services to those most vulnerable.

Finally in closing I would like to say watch out world the results of our work astounded even us, because many who went through the kind of heart work we allowed ourselves to feel would have fainted during the process.

Moving forward we are valuable human beings and will ask to be paid for the work that we know God has fully equipped us to deliver with a passion that causes a lasting transformation.